ALFRED THE KING

ISBN# 1-930710-31-3
Copyright ©2000 Veritas Press

All rights reserved. No part of this book may be reproduced or
transmitted in any form or by any means, electronic or mechanical,
including photocopying, recording, or by any information storage
and retrieval system, without permission in writing from the publisher.

Veritas Press
1250 Belle Meade Drive
Lancaster, PA 17601

First edition

ALFRED THE KING

Story by Chris Schlect
Art by Mark Ammerman

This book is dedicated to
our children.
—C.S.

Egburt was a Saxon King. His kingdom was Wessex. King Egburt had a love for God. He led his men to win a combat. With this win his kingdom was then majestic.

The men in his kingdom did submit with gladness to King Egburt. All was blissful in the kingdom of Wessex. Then the brash North Men did attack. They were quick as a

flash in long ships. The intrepid men were bad. They did rob and sack the kingdom. They did not love God.

King Egburt led his men to combat with a flag. Axes did flash, and helmets did clang. It was sad that his Saxons did not win this clash.

   From then on the North Men did trash all kingdoms of the Saxons. They did push on a trek to Essex and press on to Sussex. Then they sat in Wessex.

Athelwulf, the son of King Egburt, led his men to clash with the cads. They did push and push, but they did not push the

North Men back. It is pitiful that Athelwulf and his sons fell.

Who will abet the kingdom of Egburt and Athelwulf? Who will quell the North Men?

Who will be king? Alfred will!
 Alfred, the fifth son of Athelwulf, did not fall in combat.

Alfred did not plot to be a king. The fifth son cannot be a king. Yet, Athelwulf and his sons fell. Then fifth son can be king!

Alfred is King of Wessex! He has to win back his kingdom. Can King Alfred whip the gruff North Men?

The intrepid cads from the North were led by King Guthram. They did clash with King Alfred and his fretting men. They did grab and crush. They did trap and slit.

Clinging to the flag of King Alfred, the Saxons did zig-zag and run into the brush. Then, the men of Guthram did sit and brag of sin to their dull god.

In the hills, Alfred's men sat in a wet black glen. They sang to God and did long to fix the mess and be rid of the North Men. Glum King Alfred sat with them; but he was

ALFRED HAD A PLAN

planning a plot as he was drumming a log. He and his men were sad. Yet King Alfred had his love for God. He did not fret. He had a plan!

From the hills and on to Edington, Alfred's men ran. They ran in flits to club and slit Guthram's men with a click and clack of axes. The men of Wessex did slash, and the

North Men bled; the gravel was slick with red. The sun did slip by as Guthram and his men fled. Alfred's kingdoms did win the combat!

King Alfred and his Saxons did bless God. The cads did not crush Alfred's kingdoms of Wessex, Essex, and Sussex. Then Alfred did press Guthram to love God.

Guthram's dull god was no god. Guthram did cling to the God of Alfred. Then the North Men fled from all the Saxons in Wessex, Sussex and Essex.

Then King Alfred had a big plan to quell all North Men. He and his men set up ships. The ships were long and quick.

The ships of the North did not match Alfred's ships.

Then, King Alfred had his men bring bricks to set up walls. Brick by brick the walls were set up with slabs and slats. With all the bricks set, King Alfred and his men can rush from

the back of the walls. The men of Wessex did prep for a clash. This prep did quell the North Men.

No North Men will clash with Wessex afresh.
God did abet Alfred and his men of Wessex at Edington. King Alfred was glad for his God.

All was blissful in the kingdoms of the Saxons. All in the kingdoms sing to the God of King Alfred.